SPY
NINJAS™
NEW
RECRUITS

ISBN 978-1-338-88723-5

10 9 8 7 6 5 4 3 2 1 23 24 25 26 27

Printed in the U.S.A. 40

First printing 2023

ART BY **Mike Anderson**

EDITED BY **Lori Wieczorek**

LETTERING BY **Jeff Powell**

BOOK DESIGN BY **Nick Russell**

ART DIRECTION BY **Salena Mahina**

NEW RECRUITS

WRITTEN BY
VANNOTES

ILLUSTRATED BY
MIKE ANDERSON

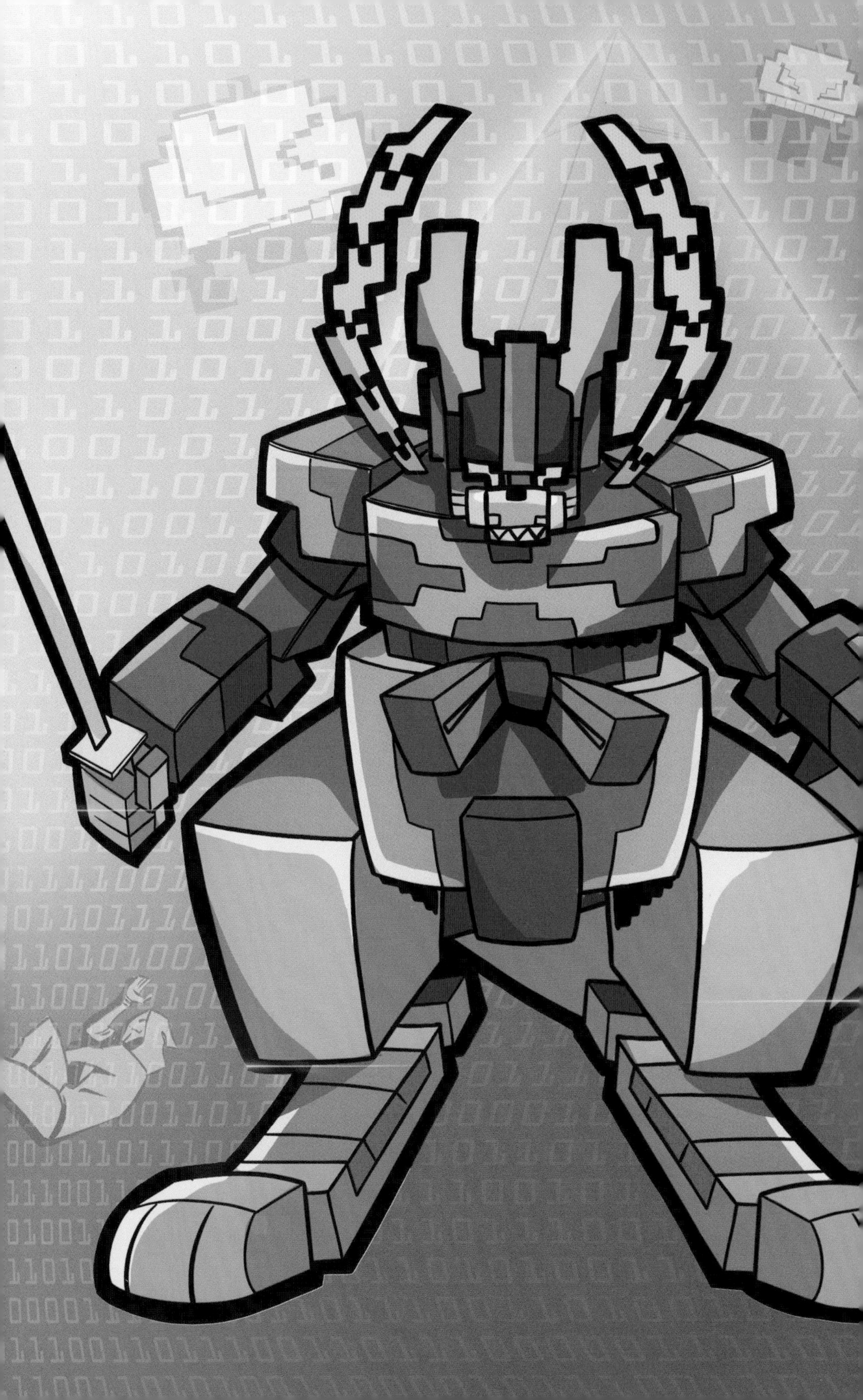

CHAPTER 1

Vy Qwaint Cam
REC
WHAT'S UP, SPY NINJAS! GUESS WHO FOUND A SECRET PROJECT ZORGO BASE, AND GUESS WHO'S TOTALLY KICKING BUTT?

SPOILER ALERT: IT'S US!
Chad Wild Clay Cam

COULD YOU WAIT A MINUTE?
REC VY REC
WE'RE FILMING A SHORT VIDEO.
IS THAT ALL OF THEM, VY?
THAT SEEMED TOO EASY, CHAD.
YOU MAY HAVE BEATEN US . . . *OUCH* . . . BUT YOU FELL FOR OUR REAL PLAN!

SORRY, CHAD AND VY, PROJECT ZORGO ARE GONNA HELP US FIND OUR PARENTS, SO WE'RE LEAVING WITH THEM.
WAIT, WHAT?! WHERE ARE YOU TAKING OUR FRIENDS?
GIVE THEM BACK!
YOU'VE MADE FOOLS OF US SO MANY TIMES AND NOW WE'VE MADE FOOLS OF YOU! YOUR FRIENDS ARE OURS NOW.
!!??
THEY'LL COME BACK . . . THEY HAVE TO.

FERNANDA "FERN" ARCIGA.
Expert hacker and gamer.
Not a Spy Ninja . . . yet.
DO DO
WOW, THAT WAS TOUGH TO WATCH.
INDEED IT WAS.

SO WHY ARE YOU SHOWING THIS TO ME AGAIN, DIRECTOR JANUS?
THIS WAS THE LAST KNOWN VIDEO SHOWING THE SPY NINJAS.
WE AT S.N.O.O.P.Z. ARE CONCERNED THAT THEY'VE GIVEN UP ON THEIR MISSION OF FIGHTING PROJECT ZORGO.
DOO
SO WHAT DOES THE SECRET NETWORK OF OPERATIVES OPPOSING PROJECT ZORGO WANT ME TO DO?
YOU ARE THE BEST HACKER WE KNOW AND A SPY NINJAS FAN TO BOOT, FIRST PLAYER FERN. WE NEED YOU TO INFILTRATE INTO THE SPY NINJAS SAFE HOUSE AND SEE WHAT'S BECOME OF THEM.

THEY PROBABLY HAVE TOP-NOTCH SECURITY. IT'LL BE A TOUGH JOB.
WE HAVE ALSO IDENTIFIED TWO OTHER INDIVIDUALS WITH TALENTS THAT MAY HELP IN THE MISSION. LIKE YOU, THEY'VE FOLLOWED THE SPY NINJAS FOR A LONG TIME.
I CAN DO THIS JOB ALONE. LIKE I ALWAYS DO.
YOU'RE A GOOD HACKER, BUT DO YOU HAVE ALL THE INFILTRATION SKILLS FOR THIS KIND OF MISSION?
WHATEVER. FINE. I EXPECT MY USUAL RATE FOR THE JOB.
AND REMEMBER, S.N.O.O.P.Z.'S WORK IS SO IMPORTANT, YOU MUST NEVER DISCUSS OUR EXISTENCE WITH ANYONE ELSE OUT LOUD.
EVEN THE SPY NINJAS!

AND THAT'S HOW YOU DO A QUADRUPLE FLIP.
REC
DREW TOM. Parkour expert and total fitness buff.
LET'S SEE HOW THAT SHOT LOOKED.
I DIDN'T KNOW PARKOUR WAS STILL COOL.
WHO ARE YOU?

THE NAME'S FERN. I'M PUTTING TOGETHER A TEAM.
HOW DID YOU FIND ME? A TEAM TO DO WHAT?
EASY. I CAN HACK ANYTHING. AND I'M LOOKING FOR SOMEONE WHO LIKES A CHALLENGE. I'M BREAKING INTO THE SPY NINJAS SAFE HOUSE!
WHOA, WHAT?! THE SPY NINJAS! CHAD WILD CLAY IS MY HERO!
DOES THIS MEAN I GET TO MEET THEM?

LATER THAT DAY...
HURRY, WILFRED! WE'VE ONLY BEEN TO FIVE OF THE TEN STORES ON MY ITINERARY TODAY. MY FOLLOWERS ARE LOOKING FORWARD TO MY UNBOXING VIDEO.
HEY THERE, ARE YOU MS. CARTER CRUZ?

OUCH!
YES. AND WHO ARE YOU?

ISN'T THE POINT OF A DISGUISE THAT PEOPLE DON'T PAY ATTENTION TO YOU?
CORRECTION: THEY PAY LESS ATTENTION THAN IF IT WERE ME!
TRINA CARTER CRUZ. Kind of famous heiress to the vast Carter Cruz fortune . . . who isn't actually an old Hollywood movie star.
WILFRED, WHAT DID I TELL YOU ABOUT USING PUBLIC WIFI? THAT'S HOW THESE HACKER TYPES ALWAYS FIND ME.
YOU TWO DON'T SEEM LIKE THE REGULAR HACKER TYPES THOUGH.
WE'RE NOT. WE NEED YOUR HELP TO INFILTRATE THE SPY NINJAS SAFE HOUSE.

WILFRED! START THE CAR. TAKE US WHEREVER THE E-GIRL SAYS.
I'D DO ANYTHING TO MEET VY QWAINT.
RIGHT ON, LITTLE BOSS DUDETTE.
I'LL FOLLOW THEM LIKE MY BOARD FOLLOWS THE CRASHING WAVE.
HE DOESN'T SEEM LIKE A REGULAR BUTLER.
MY DAD HIRED HIM BASED ON HOW BUTLER-Y HIS NAME WAS . . . WHICH WAS A HUGE MISTAKE.

SPY NINJAS SAFE HOUSE
WHAM
Property of Spy Ninjas
Property of Spy Ninjas
SCREEECH
HE IS A FAST DRIVER, AT LEAST.
AS LONG AS YOU SURVIVE THE TRIP . . .
NO DOUBT THEY USE AN ADVANCED SECURITY SYSTEM TO KEEP OUT PROJECT ZORGO.
BUT NOTHING I CAN'T HANDLE.
Control Panel

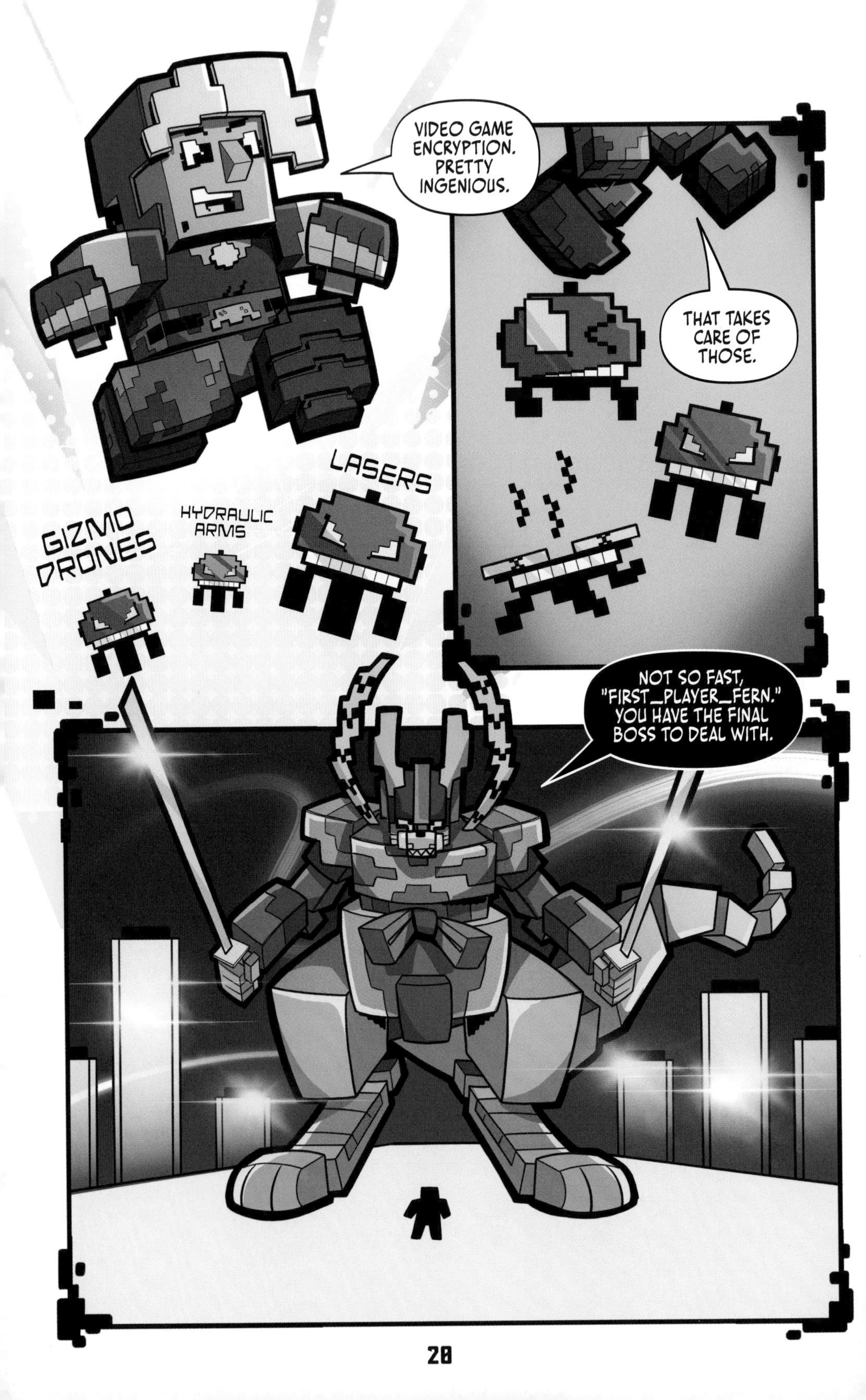
VIDEO GAME ENCRYPTION. PRETTY INGENIOUS.
LASERS
HYDRAULIC ARMS
GIZMO DRONES
THAT TAKES CARE OF THOSE.
NOT SO FAST, "FIRST_PLAYER_FERN." YOU HAVE THE FINAL BOSS TO DEAL WITH.

LET'S SEE WHO YOU REALLY ARE.
ZAP
HEY! MY CUSTOM HACKER SKIN!
HA HA HA!
WAIT! YOU'RE NOT A PROJECT ZORGO HACKER.
POOF!!
YOU'RE A KID! NICE TO MEET YA! I'M THE SPY NINJA'S BELOVED VIDEO GAME BOSS AI, SLY MARSUPIAL, NOW REPROGRAMMED TO BE A GOOD GUY AND A TOP-NOTCH SECURITY SYSTEM!

MY TEAM AND I ARE HUGE SPY NINJAS FANS AND GOT WORRIED WHEN CHAD AND VY STOPPED POSTING.
YEAH, WITHOUT THEIR SPY NINJA FRIENDS, THEY HAVEN'T LEFT THE HOUSE MUCH.
GOTTA SAY, I'M STARTING TO GET WORRIED ABOUT THOSE TWO. I CAN'T OPEN THE GATE MYSELF FOR YOU, BUT IF ONE OF YOU CAN OPEN IT FROM THE OTHER SIDE, I'VE TURNED OFF THE LASERS, BUZZSAWS, AND GIANT FALLING ANVILS. MAYBE YOU ALL CAN FINALLY CHEER UP CHAD AND VY . . .
DON'T WORRY! I'VE GOT THIS PART.

NO PROBLEM FOR THE BEST PARKOUR TRACEUR IN LAS VEGAS.
YOU'VE GOT HOPS, KID, BUT THAT'S NOT GOING TO GET YOU IN THE FRONT DOOR.

DON'T WORRY, I'VE GOT THAT PART COVERED. IT'S HARD TO SAY NO TO FAMILY.
DING DONG
DID YOU ORDER DELIVERY?
NOT TODAY.
MEXI BELL
MEXI BELL
WHO'S THERE?
CHADLEY! IT'S YOUR LONG-LOST GREAT AUNT LOLA! I'VE COME ALL THE WAY TO LAS VEGAS FROM THE CARIBBEAN TO VISIT YOU!

I HAVE A GREAT AUNT LOLA?
IS YOUR REAL NAME CHADLEY?
I DON'T THINK SO . . .
UMMM . . . HELLO, AUNT LOLA?
ANOTHER MASTERFUL PERFORMANCE FROM TRINA CARTER CRUZ!
THANK GOODNESS, IT'S JUST A BUNCH OF KIDS. I THOUGHT I'D FORGOTTEN A WHOLE AUNT.
SLY KNOWS SHE'S ONLY ALLOWED TO LET THE DELIVERY GUY PAST THE GATE!

OMG! CHAD! VY! YOU'RE ALIVE!
WHO SAID WE WEREN'T?
WE JUST HAVEN'T FELT LIKE MAKING VIDEOS LATELY . . .
WAIT, SO IF YOU'RE HERE MOPING . . .
WHO'S FIGHTING PROJECT ZORGO?
WE LOST THE REST OF OUR CREW.
SO . . . NOBODY I GUESS.

NOW IF YOU KIDS DON'T MIND, WE HAVE SOME MOPING IN OUR SWEATPANTS TO DO.
SEE YOU NEXT TIME, AUNT LOLA.
AAAAHHHH!

PLOP
WELL, THAT WAS AN EPIC FAIL.

CHAPTER
2

WOW. DOESN'T LOOK LIKE WE CAN COUNT ON THE SPY NINJAS ANY LONGER.
WHO KNEW THEY'D TURN OUT TO BE SUCH COUCH POTATOES AFTER KICKING SO MUCH BUTT? THEY MUST BE REALLY BUMMED OUT BY WHAT HAPPENED.
TAC"O"BOUT IT
TACO

TAC-O'-BOUT IT
IF THEY'RE TOO BUMMED TO FIGHT PROJECT ZORGO AND POST NEW VIDEOS . . .
WHAT AM I EVEN GOING TO WATCH IN MY FREE TIME NOW?
BESIDES TACO-EATING-CHALLENGE VIDEOS!
CHOMP
WE'LL HAVE TO GO TO MY FAVORITE FRY BREAD TRUCK NEXT. IT'S ALMOST AS GOOD AS MY GRANDMA'S.
AND A LOT BETTER THAN TRINA'S SUGGESTION OF FROG LEGS FOR LUNCH.
UGH, YOU JUST DON'T HAVE MY SOPHISTICATED PALATE, DREW.

I'M WORRIED ABOUT PROJECT ZORGO. WITHOUT THE SPY NINJAS TO KEEP THEM IN CHECK, THEY COULD SHUT DOWN THE ENTIRE INTERNET IF THEY WANTED TO.
LET'S SEE WHAT THEY'RE UP TO. HACKING PROJECT ZORGO'S SYSTEM SHOULD BE AS EASY AS FINISHING THOSE TACOS.
PROJECT ZORGO'S SECURITY SEEMS WAY LESS FUN THAN THE SPY NINJA'S WAS.
PEW PEW PEW
ALL IT WILL TAKE IS A FEW WELL-PLACED SHOTS AT PROJECT ZORGO'S ANTIVIRUS SOFTWARE TO GET IN.

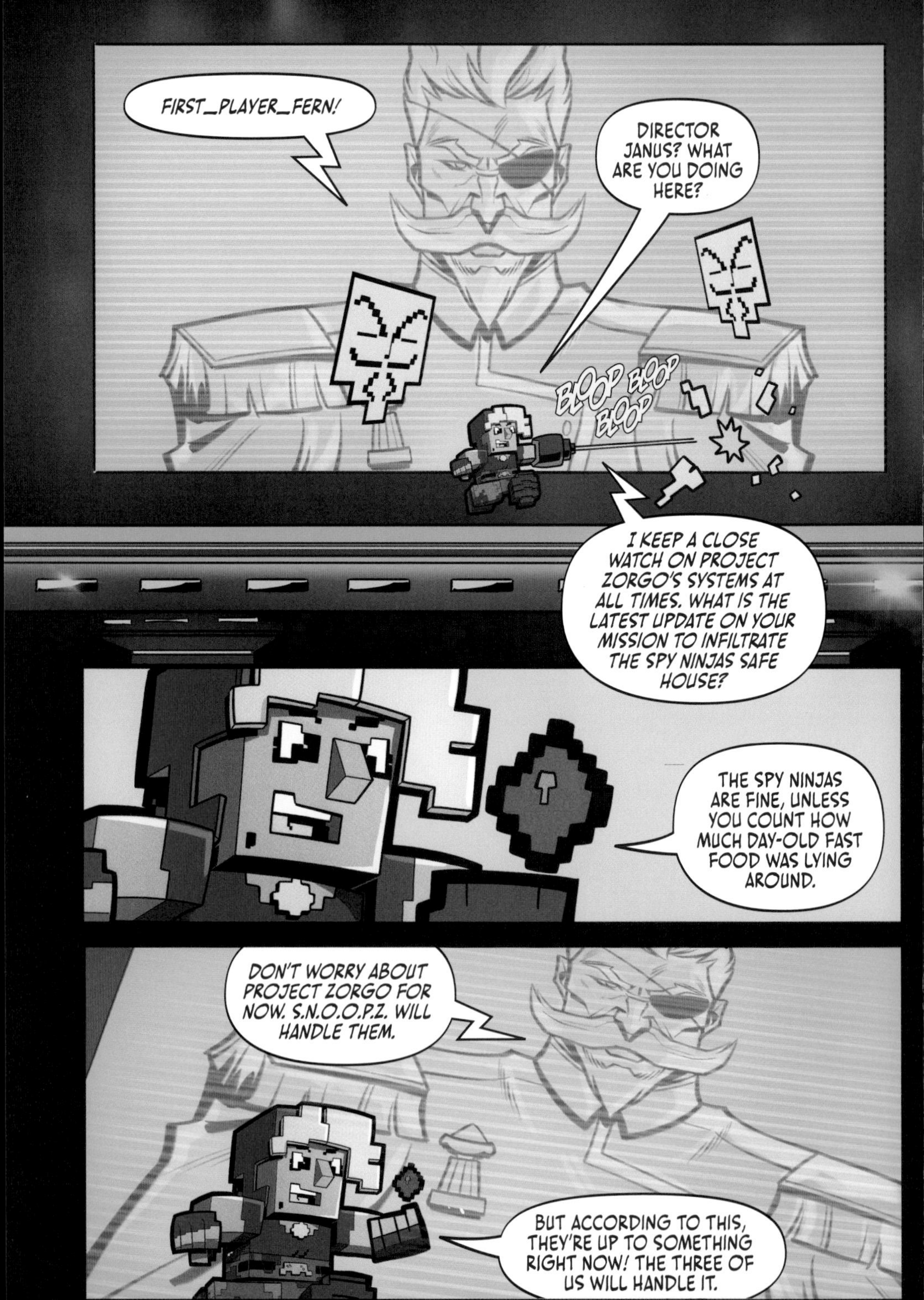
FIRST_PLAYER_FERN!
DIRECTOR JANUS? WHAT ARE YOU DOING HERE?
BLOOP BLOOP BLOOP
I KEEP A CLOSE WATCH ON PROJECT ZORGO'S SYSTEMS AT ALL TIMES. WHAT IS THE LATEST UPDATE ON YOUR MISSION TO INFILTRATE THE SPY NINJAS SAFE HOUSE?
THE SPY NINJAS ARE FINE, UNLESS YOU COUNT HOW MUCH DAY-OLD FAST FOOD WAS LYING AROUND.
DON'T WORRY ABOUT PROJECT ZORGO FOR NOW. S.N.O.O.P.Z. WILL HANDLE THEM.
BUT ACCORDING TO THIS, THEY'RE UP TO SOMETHING RIGHT NOW! THE THREE OF US WILL HANDLE IT.

WHO WERE YOU TALKING TO? ANOTHER VIDEO GAME KANGAROO?
OH . . . I TALK TO MYSELF A LOT WHILE PLAYING VIDEO GAMES . . .
SO WHERE IS PROJECT ZORGO STRIKING NEXT?
PROJECT ZORGO'S NEXT SCHEME IS BRINGING A TRUCK OF HIGH-TECH EQUIPMENT INTO LAS VEGAS TONIGHT.

WE'LL INTERCEPT THAT TRUCK AND SHOW PROJECT ZORGO WHAT WE'RE CAPABLE OF!
I'LL LIVE STREAM THE WHOLE OPERATION. MAYBE SEEING US IN ACTION WILL INSPIRE THE SPY NINJAS.
WILFRED, BRING THE CAR AROUND. WE'VE GOT A MISSION TO PREPARE FOR.
YOU GOT IT, BOSS DUDETTE!
MIND IF I FINISH MY TACOS, THOUGH?
TACO 'BOUT IT

DID YOU SEE THE ONE WITH THE CAT WHO WEARS LITTLE DINOSAUR OUTFITS?
YEAH. DID YOU SEE THE VIDEO OF THE CAKE THAT LOOKS LIKE A TOILET?
YEAH, DID YOU . . .
THE SPY NINJAS ALERT SYSTEM?
ALERT
!!!
WAIT. . .?
HI, TRINA TOTS! IT'S YOUR GIRL TRINA CC HERE WITH A SPECIAL LIVE EVENT ALONG WITH FIRST_PLAYER_FERN AND DREW TOM, AKA THE KING OF THE LAS VEGAS PARKOUR SCENE!
REC
OH NO. IT'S THOSE KIDS!
THIS CAN'T BE GOOD.

APPROACHING THE SHIPMENT.
ZORGO
VRRRRRMMMMMM

THEY CAN'T BE SERIOUS!
A HIGH-SPEED CHASE?!
WE NEED TO STOP THEM BEFORE THEY GET HURT!
CHAD IS PRETTY GOOD AT STUNTS, BUT CAN HE DO . . .
THIS!

TOO EASY.
PROJECT ZORGO HACKERS.
Good at grunt work. Okay at driving.
THUMP THUMP THUMP
???
WHAT WAS THAT?
NO WAY!

MIND IF I TAG ALONG FOR THE RIDE?
BAM
POW
BIFF
BASED ON THEIR LIVE FEED, I'VE TRIANGULATED THEIR POSITION.
LET'S HOPE WE'RE NOT TOO LATE.

OKAY, TRINA TOTS! NOW THAT DREW'S STOPPED THE TRUCK AND CAPTURED THE HACKER DRIVER, LET'S GET A PEEK AT WHAT PROJECT ZORGO WAS TRYING TO SMUGGLE INTO LAS VEGAS.
WELL, THAT'S NOT CREEPY.
PROJECT ZORGO IS TOTALLY OBSESSED WITH THE SPY NINJAS.

IT'S LIKE THEY COULD WAKE UP AT ANY MOMENT . . .
INTERLOPERS DETECTED! INITIATE DEFENSE PROTOCOLS.
YIKES!
FWOOOSH
Y'KNOW, THAT'S A BIT MORE WHAT I THOUGHT MEETING VY WOULD BE LIKE . . .

INTERLOPERS DETECTED! INITIATE DEFENSE PROTOCOLS.

DON'T WORRY, TRINA TOTS! FERN'S GOING TO HACK THESE ROBOTS.
I CAN'T HACK ANYTHING INSTANTLY, TRINA!
THIS MIGHT BE MY LAST VIDEO, BUT LIKE AND SUBSCRIBE JUST IN CASE!

STEP BACK, KIDS! THIS IS A JOB FOR THE SPY NINJAS.
LOOKS LIKE THEIR WIRING ISN'T UP TO CODE YET.
ZAP

SPY NINJAS DETECTED.
PRIME DIRECTIVE: KEEP OPERATION "SHINOBI ARMY" SECRET.
ESCAPE PROTOCOL ENGAGED.
RETURN TO THE TRUCK! RETURN TO THE TRUCK! RETURN TO THE TRUCK!

VRRRRRMMMM
WE CAN STILL CATCH THEM!
I'M NOT SO SURE ABOUT THAT, VY . . .
VRRRRREEEE

UGH! THEY GOT AWAY FROM US.
ON OUR OWN BIKES!
WAIT A MINUTE, IF THEY'RE US AND THEY STEAL OUR BIKES, BUT THEY'RE NOT US, BUT THEY HAVE OUR FACES, WOULD THEY TECHNICALLY BE STEALING IF THEY'RE . . .
UGH, THAT'S WAY TOO CONFUSING TO THINK ABOUT.
AND YOU THREE! WHAT WERE YOU DOING? YOU COULD HAVE GOTTEN KILLED!
WE WERE DOING MORE THAN YOU TWO WERE.

WHEN WAS THE LAST TIME YOU TWO DID A HIGH-SPEED CHASE?
OR HACKED THE PROJECT ZORGO NETWORK?
NOT SINCE . . .
THE WHOLE TEAM WAS TOGETHER.
SO YOU THREE WANT TO BE SPY NINJAS?
LET'S SEE IF YOU'VE GOT WHAT IT TAKES.

CHAPTER
3

YOU HAVE A NEW MISSION, FIRST_PLAYER_FERN.
S.N.O.O.P.Z. IS STILL CONCERNED ABOUT THE WELLNESS OF THE SPY NINJAS. WE WANT VIDEO OF THEM IN ACTION.
MY CONTACTS SHOULD BE GIVING YOU A LIVE FEED AS WE SPEAK.
WE HAVE HEARD PROJECT ZORGO'S PLANS ARE COMMENCING IN THREE DAYS. WE WILL RENDEZVOUS WITH YOU AT THEIR BLACK PYRAMID BASE.
UNDERSTOOD.
WHAT ARE YOU DOING IN HERE, WEIRDO?

WE'RE ABOUT TO GET STARTED!

OKAY, FIRST GROUND RULE OF SPY NINJA TRAINING: NO HANGING OUT IN OUR CLOSET WITHOUT PERMISSION.
SPY NINJAS ADVANCED TRAINING: DAY 1
THERE'S A LOT OF SHARP STUFF IN THERE.

VY AND I AREN'T SOLD ON TAKING ON MORE TEAM MEMBERS YET, BUT WE DO NEED YOU THREE TO HELP US WITH WHATEVER PROJECT ZORGO IS PLANNING.
EVEN ME?
WE'LL DEFINITELY BE NEEDING YOU TO DRIVE US AROUND UNTIL WE GET NEW WHEELS.
CHAD AND I WILL TRAIN YOU OVER THE NEXT THREE DAYS.
NOW, WHO'S READY FOR DAY ONE?

FIRST! YOU MUST MASTER THE MAZE OF TRAMPOLINES!
THIS IS RIDICULOUS. WHAT DOES THIS HAVE TO DO WITH BEATING UP BAD GUYS?
TRAMPOLINES ARE THE ULTIMATE TEST OF SPRINGINESS, AND MAZES ARE THE ULTIMATE TEST OF SMARTYNESS.

I'VE NEVER BEEN SO BAD AT STUNTS BEFORE . . .
SECOND! YOU MUST UNDERSTAND FINESSE WITH A WEAPON.
WHICH IS BEST MASTERED THROUGH THE ART OF SLICING FRUIT IN MIDAIR!
I'M NOT SURE THEY LEARNED HOW TO USE KATANAS BY SLICING WATERMELONS IN ANCIENT JAPAN . . .
SLICE
A KATANA TRULY IS THE ONLY WAY TO SLICE YOUR FRUIT.

THIRD! A SPY NINJA MUST BE A MASTER OF VIDEO GAMES!
EWW, GET THESE FLIES AWAY FROM ME.
FINALLY! SOMETHING I'M GOOD AT!
WAIT A MINUTE! WHAT THE SPOOF IS THIS?
KEI TRUCK SIMULATOR! THE ENTIRE GOAL IS TO NAVIGATE A LITTLE TRUCK THROUGH THE TIGHT STREETS OF JAPAN WITHOUT DROPPING YOUR PLUMS! DOESN'T THAT SOUND FUN?
WHERE ARE THE EXPLOSIONS?!

DID THAT DAY REALLY HAPPEN?
WERE WE JUST PRANKED?
HOW DOES DRIVING A VIDEO GAME TRUCK TRAIN US TO FIGHT PROJECT ZORGO?
I COULDN'T GET THROUGH TO THEM, VY.
YOU'RE GOOD WITH PEOPLE. MAYBE YOU CAN REACH THEM.
IF WE CAN'T TEACH THEM WITH FUN, THEN WE'LL TEACH THEM WITH TOUGH LOVE.

ARE YOU SURE YOU DON'T NEED A RIDE, FERN?
DON'T WORRY, I LIVE A COUPLE BLOCKS OVER.
beep beep beep
WAS THAT DATA SUFFICIENT FOR YOU?
WE ARE STILL NOT CONVINCED.
TO BE HONEST, NEITHER AM I . . .

SPY NINJAS ADVANCED TRAINING: DAY 2
ALL RIGHT, RECRUITS! IT SOUNDS LIKE CHAD WENT TOO EASY ON YOU ALL.
THAT MEANS IT'S FALLEN ON ME TO KNOCK SOME SENSE INTO YOU.
TODAY'S WHEN THE REAL TRAINING BEGINS.

FIRST, YOU MUST HAVE PEAK UPPER BODY STRENGTH.
AND IMPECCABLE BALANCE.
OOOF!
A HUNDRED MORE PUSHUPS FOR YOU, MS. CARTER CRUZ!

SECOND! RUNNING! A SPY NINJA MUST BE ABLE TO RUN IN AND OUT OF ANY DANGEROUS SITUATION.
WHILE AVOIDING OBSTACLES.
SPLAT
SPLAT
SPLAT
YOU CAN'T STOP RUNNING UNTIL YOU'RE ABSOLUTELY DRY! YOU CAN DO IT!

THIRD! BEING A SPY NINJA ISN'T ONLY ABOUT PHYSICAL STRENGTH.
Disguise Cream
Ninja Makeup
THANK GOODNESS! SOMETHING I'M FINALLY GOOD AT.
A SPY NINJA MUST BE ABLE TO CAMOUFLAGE THEMSELVES IN HOSTILE TERRAIN.
AND WELL ENOUGH TO AVOID THE FACIAL RECOGNITION ON THE SPY NINJAS LASER GRID.

THAT WAS EVEN WORSE THAN YESTERDAY.
I CAN BARELY MOVE. EVEN MY HAIR HURTS.
BEEP BEEP BEEP
DO YOU NEED TO GET THAT?
Um . . . NO, IT'S JUST SOME TROUBLESHOOTING NOTIFICATIONS FOR NEW CODE I'M DEVELOPING. SUPER BORING.
THWACK SMACK CHOP
WAIT, WHAT'S THAT?
ANY LUCK WITH THEM TODAY?

NO BETTER THAN YOU. I GUESS THE DRILL SERGEANT ROUTINE DIDN'T WORK.

THEY'RE STILL NOT READY TO GO TOE-TO-TOE WITH PROJECT ZORGO.
MAYBE WE DO HAVE TO BENCH THEM FOR THE MISSION TOMORROW.
WAIT A MINUTE! YOU CAN'T BENCH US!
HEAR ME OUT! INSTEAD OF TRYING TO TRAIN US TO BATTLE PROJECT ZORGO, MAYBE YOU SHOULD START AT THE BEGINNING AND TEACH US HOW TO BECOME SPY NINJAS.

THAT'S . . . A GOOD IDEA. I THINK WE CAN MAKE THAT WORK, RIGHT, VY?
I'LL PUT AWAY THE PLUNGECHUCK. CHAD IS THE NUNCHUCK EXPERT ANYWAY.
OKAY, WE'VE GOT ONE LAST DAY TO GET READY. VY AND I HAVEN'T BEEN GREAT TEACHERS, BUT GIVE US ONE LAST CHANCE.

BEEP BEEP
BEEP BEEP
BEEP BEEP
BEEP BEEP
WHAT IS IT?
YOU'VE BEEN IGNORING MY CALLS. ARE YOU TRULY PREPARED FOR THE MISSION TOMORROW?
I GUESS. HEY, WHY HAVEN'T CHAD AND VY EVER TALKED ABOUT S.N.O.O.P.Z. IN ANY OF OUR MEETINGS?
THEY MUST NOT WANT TO REVEAL OUR IDENTITY TO THE OTHER TWO NEW RECRUITS.
YOU'RE A KEY PART OF S.N.O.O.P.Z.'S PLAN TO STOP PROJECT ZORGO, FIRST_PLAYER_FERN. DON'T LET US DOWN.

WE DID WHAT YOU ASKED.
VY AND I WROTE DOWN ALL THE THINGS WE WISH WE KNEW WHEN WE BECAME SPY NINJAS. IT ALL STARTED WITH BEING A GREAT YOUTUBER!
NOTES
Teamwork
Weapons
Fruit Slicing
Video Making
Online Safety
ARE YOU READY TO LEARN THE ACTUAL TACTICS OF BEING A SPY NINJA?
FINALLY!
LET'S GET TO THE REAL TRAINING, THEN!

TIP 1: Your viewers will have more fun if you're having fun!
TIP 2: Create a list of video ideas and pick one.
Making the most EPIC pizza with only our ninja weapons!!

TIP 3: Get creative! Use items lying around the house as props.
TIP 4: Be ready to work hard! Creating videos isn't always easy.

TIP 5: Be yourself. You don't need to worry about impressing other people.
#1 DAD
TIP 6: The quality of your equipment isn't very important. A good video can be made with even an old phone.

TIP 7: Create a title and thumbnail for your videos that make people curious to click.
PIZZA IN A CAN

TIP 8: Always have somebody you trust review your video BEFORE posting it.

TIP 9: Everybody gets mean comments, so don't feel too bad. Try to ignore the haters.

TIP 10: HAVE FUN!
Your viewers will have more fun if you're having fun!

SO HOW DID YOU BECOME A BUTLER?
ONLINE BUTLER UNIVERSITY OF COURSE.
HOW LONG WAS THAT PROGRAM?
LIKE AN HOUR, TOPS.
BEEP BEEP
Have you left the safe house yet?
I know.
YOU OKAY, FERN?
WE'VE BEEN HAVING SO MUCH FUN TODAY AND YOU JUST LOOKED BUMMED OUT ALL OF A SUDDEN.

IT'S NOTHING! JUST NERVOUS FOR TONIGHT'S MISSION.
I CAN'T SHAKE THIS WEIRD FEELING, THOUGH.
IF YOU NEED ANYTHING, WE'RE A TEAM NOW.
WE'RE HERE TO HELP EACH OTHER.
WWEEEOOOOOOWEEEOOO
PROJECT ZORGO IS MAKING THEIR MOVE.
TIME TO SEE IF THE LAST THREE DAYS' TRAINING PAID OFF.

CHAPTER
4

THE BLACK PYRAMID, AKA PROJECT ZORGO HEADQUARTERS . . . which no one in Las Vegas seems to notice at all.

VROOOOMM
ALL RIGHT, TEAM, OPERATION: FAMILY VACATION IS ABOUT TO BEGIN. THANKS FOR THE EXCELLENT DISGUISES, TRINA.
YOU'RE WELCOME!
I ♥ VEGAS

ARE YOU SURE WE CAN'T WEAR OUR NORMAL CLOTHES?
IT'S A DISGUISE. YOU'LL GET TO DITCH IT SOON.
SCREECH
WE'RE HERE! GOOD LUCK, DUDES AND DUDETTES!

FIGURES. IT'S THE BIG NIGHT AND THEY STICK ME AT RECEPTION.
IT'S NOT LIKE THE SPY NINJAS ARE GOING TO WALK IN THE FRONT DOOR.
THIS MUST BE OUR HOTEL! WHAT A NEATORIFIC PLACE TO STAY ON OUR VACATION!
???
WAIT A MINUTE. YOU'VE GOT THE WRONG PLACE. YOU WANT THE PYRAMID A FEW BLOCKS . . .
STACEE

I AM ABSOLUTELY, POSITIVELY DIDDLY SURE! THE BLACK PYRAMID, IT SAYS!
STACEE
SIR, WE ARE NOT A HOTEL.
STACEE
CAN YOU BRING MY BAGS UP TO MY ROOM, KIDDO? MY ARMS ARE SO TIRED.
CAN YOU TAKE MY LOLLI, TOO? THANKS A MILLION.
EWWWW!!!

I ABSOLUTELY DIDDLY CAN'T BELIEVE THAT WORKED.
I ♥ VEGAS
NOW THAT WE'RE IN THE BUILDING, WE CAN TRACE THE SIGNAL I GOT FROM ONE OF THE ROBOTS.
LOOKS LIKE WE'RE HEADED DOWN.

YOU'VE GOT IT.
DAYS WITHOUT A SPY NINJAS INFILTRATION
92
I'M GOING TO HAVE TO ASK THE FRONT DESK ABOUT OUR ACCOMMODATIONS.
HAND
FEET
NEW MONSTER IDEA #14576
MISSING!!

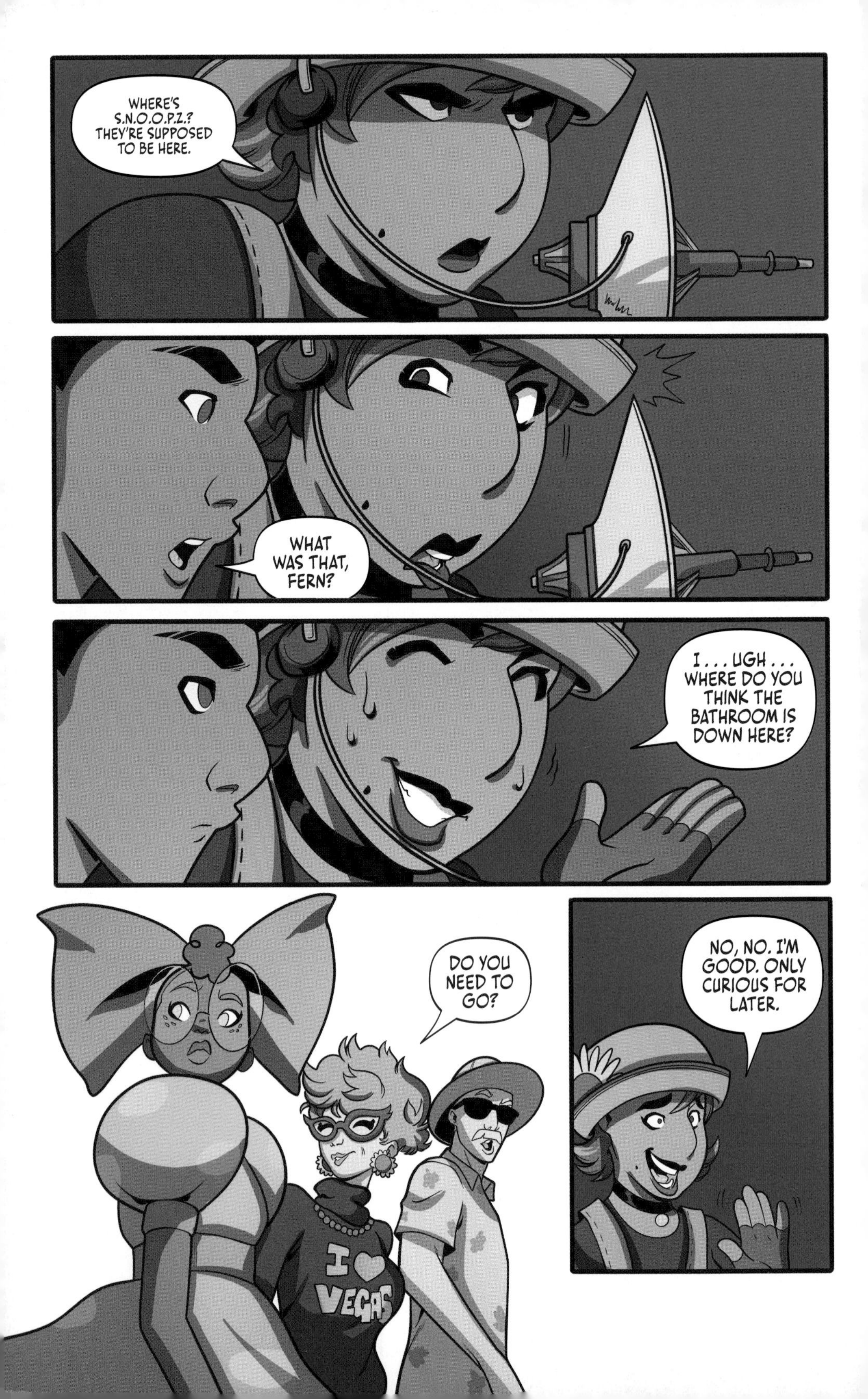
WHERE'S S.N.O.O.P.Z.? THEY'RE SUPPOSED TO BE HERE.
WHAT WAS THAT, FERN?
I . . . UGH . . . WHERE DO YOU THINK THE BATHROOM IS DOWN HERE?
DO YOU NEED TO GO?
NO, NO. I'M GOOD. ONLY CURIOUS FOR LATER.
I ♥ VEGAS

WOW, HOW MANY OF THEM ARE THERE?
ENOUGH FOR YEARS OF UNBOXING VIDEOS.

WHAT A DELIGHTFUL LITTLE FAMILY.
YOU'RE RIGHT, WE'RE DELIGHTFUL AND WE'RE ABOUT TO HAVE A GREAT TIME DEMOLISHING THIS LAB.
I'M SORRY, BUT IT LOOKS LIKE YOU'LL BE CHECKING OUT SOON.
WE'VE STOPPED YOUR EVIL PLANS BEFORE. WHAT DO YOU THINK WILL MAKE THIS TIME ANY DIFFERENT?
YOU'RE RIGHT! WE'VE NEVER BEEN ABLE TO BEAT YOU.

THAT'S WHY WE DEVELOPED OUR LATEST EVIL WEAPONS TO BE AS GOOD AS YOU TWO ARE.
OH NO . . .
KEEP YOUR COOL, TEAM, AND BE READY FOR ANYTHING.

TBH, I DON'T THINK MAKING PIZZA PREPARED ME FOR THIS.

WAIT JUST A MINUTE, MY CHADROIDS AND VYBOTS.
THERE'S ONE AMONG THEM WHO HAS DONE A GREAT DEAL TO ASSIST US. THE ONE WHO COLLECTED THE RAW DATA OF CHAD WILD CLAY AND VY QWAINT'S SPY NINJAS TECHNIQUES.
JOIN ME, FIRST_PLAYER_FERN.
YOU! YOU WERE DIRECTOR JANUS?!
FERN!
WHAT'S GOING ON?!

I CAN'T BELIEVE I FELL FOR THEIR SCHEME. I'M . . . I'M SUPPOSED TO BE THE SMART ONE.
I'VE BETRAYED . . .
. . . THE ONLY TEAM I'VE EVER KNOWN.
I CAN'T BELIEVE WE'VE BEEN INFILTRATED AGAIN.
HOW DOES THIS ALWAYS HAPPEN?
NOW THAT WE'VE HAD A PROPER DOUBLE CROSS . . .

LET THE PUMMELING COMMENCE.

UGH! THEY DO KNOW ALL OF OUR MOVES.
AND THERE'S TOO MANY OF THEM!
CHOP
OOOOW!

TIME TO RECYCLE SOME TIN CANS!
HEY, WAIT! WE'RE GOOD AT FIGHTING, TOO!
THE BOTS DON'T CARE ABOUT US AT ALL.
WE'VE GOT TO GET DREW AND TRINA TO SAFETY!
RIGHT.

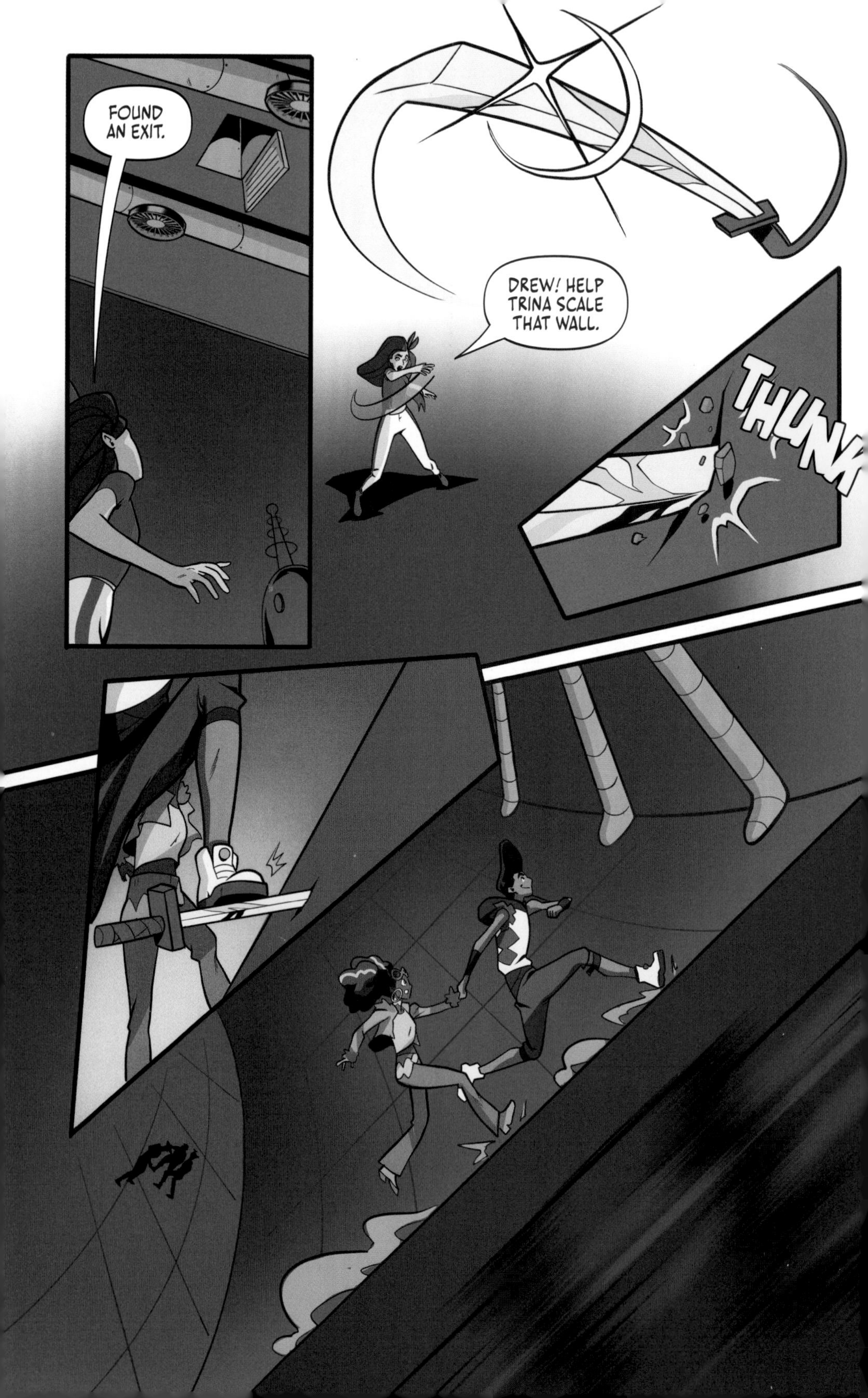
FOUND AN EXIT.
DREW! HELP TRINA SCALE THAT WALL.
THUNK

STILL THINK PARKOUR ISN'T COOL ENOUGH FOR YOUR SOCIAL FEED?
OH NO!
THEY HARDLY LASTED A MINUTE.
WE WOULD HAVE HAD NO CHANCE IF THEY TURNED ON US.
FWOOSH

FINALLY! THE LAST TWO SPY NINJAS DEFEATED ONCE AND FOR ALL! THE SPY NINJAS ARE NO MORE!

CHAPTER 5

THIS IS SO GROSS. I'M GETTING DUST ALL OVER MY NICE WORKOUT GEAR.
ARE YOU REALLY THINKING ABOUT YOUR CLOTHES RIGHT NOW? I'LL BUY YOU A NEW SET ONCE THIS IS OVER.
I'M HOLDING YOU TO THAT.
IF WE MAKE IT OUT OF HERE IN ONE PIECE.
DON'T WORRY. WE'LL GET OUT OF HERE SOMEHOW. WITH CHAD AND VY!

FIRST, WE NEED TO MAKE A PLAN.
I HAVE ONE.
YOU!
YOU BETRAYED US! WE WERE SUPPOSED TO BE A TEAM!!
HOLD IT, TRINA.
WHAT MAKES YOU THINK WE WANT YOUR HELP?

I THOUGHT I WAS DOING THE RIGHT THING. PROJECT ZORGO TRICKED ME THE SAME WAY THEY TRICKED CHAD AND VY AND THE OTHER MEMBERS OF THE SPY NINJAS TEAM.
NOW I KNOW HOW AWFUL THEY MUST HAVE FELT.
I SHOULDN'T HAVE TRUSTED SOME WEIRD STRANGER I MET OVER THE INTERNET.
IT'S EASY TO LET PEOPLE NLINE TRICK YOU. I ET IT. SO IF YOU'VE GOT A PLAN, THEN YOU'RE BACK ON THE TEAM.
OH, TRUST ME, I'VE GOT A PLAN.

I DISCOVERED THESE PROJECT ZORGO EXPERIMENTS WHEN I HACKED THEIR SYSTEM.
ROCKET BOOTS SHOULD HELP YOU PULL OFF A FEW NEW TRICKS.
AND A HOLOGRAPHIC HEADBAND FOR THE MASTER OF DISGUISE.
I NEED TIME, BUT I MIGHT BE ABLE TO HIT PROJECT ZORGO'S MAIN SERVER AND TAKE OUT ALL THE CHADROIDS AND VYBOTS.
THEN WE'LL GET YOU ALL THE TIME YOU NEED.

YOU'RE JUST IN TIME FOR THE GRAND FINALE.
SOON CHADROIDS AND VYBOTS WILL BE UNLEASHED ON THE WORLD TO DO THE BIDDING OF PROJECT ZORGO!
WE'LL GET OUT OF HERE SOMEHOW.
AND WHEN WE DO, THOSE ROBOTS DON'T HAVE A CHANCE!

EXCUSE ME, YOUR SCIENTIFIC-NESS, BUT I JUST RECEIVED THESE EVIL REPORTS YOU NEED TO LOOK AT RIGHT AWAY ...
WHAT'S THIS?

THEY DESCRIBE HOW YOU'RE ABOUT TO GET YOUR BUTT KICKED!
HUH?
YOUR FAVORITE MASTER OF DISGUISE IS AT THE RESCUE.
HOW DARE YOU USE MY OWN TECHNOLOGY AGAINST ME!
MIND IF I BORROW THAT?

MY FRIEND NEEDS IT MORE THAN YOU DO.
DO YOUR THING, FERN!
GOOD THING I HAVE THE RIGHT ADAPTER.
TIME TO FINALLY BEAT THIS LEVEL.

CHAD! VY! FERN IS ON OUR SIDE. PROTECT HER AT ALL COSTS WHILE SHE'S DOING HER THING!

LET'S FIND THAT SOURCE CODE!
THERE YOU ARE, FIRST_PLAYER_FERN!
YIKES!

THOSE ROBOTS KNOW ALL OF CHAD AND VY'S MOVES.
BUT THEY DON'T KNOW ANY OF OURS.
TIME FOR SOME COMBO MOVES, THEN.
COMBO MOVES?
I NEVER THOUGHT OF THAT!

JUMP, DREW!
KATANA JUMP TORNADO!

LET'S SEE IF YOU CAN KEEP YOUR EYES ON ME.
HI THERE!
HOLA!
I LIKE YOUR SHOES!
CONFUSION STUN CHUCK COMBO!

DATA UPLOAD ALMOST COMPLETE.
GAME OVER, FIRST_PLAYER_FERN!
DON'T WORRY. I HAVE MORE PLAYERS JOINING THE GAME.
WHAT DO YOU MEAN?

THANKS TO ALL THE ESPIONAGE I DID FOR YOU, I ALSO HAVE CHAD AND VY'S COMBAT DATA.
AND I DON'T THINK YOUR SYSTEM CAN TAKE THIS LEVEL OF DIFFICULTY.
NOOOOOOOO!

HEY, TEAM! WE'RE GOING TO WANT TO GET OUT OF HERE FAST!
I MIGHT HAVE ACCIDENTALLY LAUNCHED THE "SELF-DESTRUCT" PROGRAM RATHER THAN THE "TURN EVERYTHING OFF" PROGRAM.
DID SHE SAY SELF-DESTRUCT?!
THERE'S NO CHANCE OF GOING BACK UP THE WAY WE CAME DOWN.
I'VE GOT THIS! EVERYONE, LINK UP!

BOOOOMMM

ALMOST THERE! JUST A LITTLE MORE!
WE HAD A WING-DING WONDERFUL STAY!
SORRY ABOUT THE MESS WE LEFT IN THE ROOM.

WILFRED! START THE LIMO!
RIGHT ON, BOSS DUDETTE!
SCREEEEECCH

BOOOOMMMM

WOW! WHAT A SHOW!
CAN ONLY SEE SOMETHING LIKE THIS IN VEGAS!
I ♥ VEGAS
THAT WAS AWESOME! WHAT EXCITING ADVENTURE ARE WE OFF TO NEXT?
TO BED!
WAIT, WHAT HAPPENED TO ALL THOSE HACKERS? DID THEY ALL JUST—?
DON'T WORRY ABOUT THEM.

THEY ALWAYS MAKE IT OUT ALL RIGHT.
I TOLD YOU THAT WOULDN'T WORK.
IT ALMOST DID! IF THOSE ANNOYING BRATS HADN'T BEEN IN THE WAY.
MAYBE YOU ALL WILL TAKE MY SUGGESTIONS WITH THE NEXT PYRAMID AND NOT ADD A PUBLIC LOBBY.
STACEE
WE GET IT ALREADY, PZ 228. IT WAS A BAD IDEA. YOU WERE RIGHT!

A FEW DAYS LATER . . .
DID THEY SAY WHY THEY WANTED TO MEET US HERE?
NO, THEY ONLY SENT ME THEIR LOCATION.
HEY, TEAM.
GLAD YOU COULD MAKE IT.
WE WANTED TO SHOW YOU OUR NEW SPY NINJAS HEADQUARTERS.

WHOA!
THIS IS SO AWESOME!
TRÈS CHIC!
YOU THREE MADE US REALIZE THAT WE CAN'T FIGHT PROJECT ZORGO ALONE.
AND NEITHER SHOULD YOU.
THAT'S WHY WE'RE GOING TO EXPAND OUR ROSTER . . . A LOT.
ARE YOU READY TO COMPETE IN THE SPY NINJAS TRYOUTS? FOR THE MISSIONS WHERE WE CAN'T DO IT ON OUR OWN?

OF COURSE!

THEN LET'S GET TRAINING.

THE END OF ONE ADVENTURE . . . AND THE START OF EVEN MORE!

CHAD WILD CLAY

CHAD WILD CLAY is a YouTuber who learned martial arts at a young age and developed an affinity for slicing fruits with ninja gadgets. After a hacker illegally deleted a handful of his videos, Chad and Vy Qwaint formed the Spy Ninjas in order to stop the evil Project Zorgo from hacking the rest of YouTube. Using his height, speed, and strength, he can fight his way out of any situation, especially when he has his stun-chucks in hand. Although his impressive martial arts and ninja skills make him an incredible fighter, he lives his life promoting kindness, self-defense, and lighthearted humor.

VY QWAINT is co-founder of the Spy Ninjas and the tiniest member of the team. She puts her fashion and beauty vlogging on hold to battle the evil Project Zorgo and prevent them from ruining the internet. Also known as "The Spicy Spy Ninja," she is always prepared to go head-to-head with evil hackers, using her stealth, spy skills, and small size to outwit them. On the surface, Vy is petite, giggly, and silly, but don't let that fool you! Her ability to throw kicks, solve difficult puzzles, and pick even the hardest of locks make her a force to be reckoned with.

VANNOTES

VANNOTES is a writer, cartoonist, and educator based out of Idaho. Their previous work includes *Bendy: Crack-Up Comics Collection*, along with publications from Scholastic, King Features Syndicate, and Boom! Studios. They received their Bachelor of Fine Arts in Comic Art from the Minneapolis College of Art and Design and their master of fine arts in creative writing from Eastern Oregon University. They were named Treasure Valley Community College's Student Advocate of the Year in 2021. In their free time, they read way too many comics and play far too many video games.

MIKE ANDERSON

MIKE is a comic book artist from Oklahoma, where he lives with his wife, Heather, and three sons, Colt, Koda, and Caden. Mike has done work for several indie and mainstream comic publishers, as well as illustration and animation work for many national brands. Born and raised on the '80s and '90s craze of Ninja Turtles, Mike was all too excited to work on the Spy Ninjas graphic novel. When he is not drawing comics, Mike enjoys playing with his kids, animating, and scarfing lots of pizza! You can find more of his work at mikeycomix.com.